our
generation.

This is Eva's story.

EVA®

THE MYSTERY OF THE VANISHING COIN

BY

SUSAN CAPPADONIA LOVE

ILLUSTRATED BY KRISTI VALIANT

An Our Generation® *book*

MAISON JOSEPH BATTAT LTD. *Publisher*

A very special thanks to the editor,
Joanne Burke Casey.

Our Generation® Books is a registered trademark of Maison Joseph Battat Ltd.
Text copyright © 2009 by Susan Love

ISBN: 978-0-9883165-1-5
Printed in China

For Scott, Sophie and Olivia,
with love

Read all the adventures in the
Our Generation® Book Series

Read more about **Our Generation®** books and dolls online:
www.ogdolls.com

CONTENTS

EXTRA! EXTRA! READ ALL ABOUT IT!

*Big words, wacky words, powerful words, funny words...
what do they all mean? They are marked with this symbol * .
Look them up in the Glossary at the end of this book.*

Chapter One

FUMBLEFINGERS STRIKES AGAIN

"You made front page news, Eva!" My friend Bryce spread our school newspaper on the café table in front of us.

Nancy gave me the thumbs-up. "You must be so excited that *The Scoop* printed your article about the garbage problem here in Whistle Creek."

"Nice shot," Cole said, pointing to a photo of a trash can overflowing with Perk Up Coffee Shop cups and Finn's Fast Food containers.

I tried not to look too proud, but on the inside I was. My friends know my two favorite things are: #1, doing detective work with my dog Choo, and #2, writing and taking photos for *The Scoop*'s community section.

I also write an advice column called "Dear Me!" but nobody knows about it. It's by me, for me—and for my eyes only. I tell myself my problems. I give myself advice.

Sounds silly, but somehow it helps me figure things out.

Donna tapped me on the shoulder. "Don't forget, we're definitely going to the mall on Saturday. You said you'd help me find a special birthday present for my Aunt Lillian, right?"

Before I could answer, our waitress, Dottie, appeared at our table carrying a round tray. On it was our favorite ooohy-gooey melt-in-your-mouth dessert.

"Sweet!" exclaimed Cole.

"Yuuuuummmm," whispered Nancy in one long breath.

"Deeeeee-lish," I squealed as I set my camera down and put *The Scoop* aside. I unrolled my paper napkin wrapped around plastic silverware.

Choo, my detective dachshund*, got a whiff of the cake and licked her chops*. Wherever I go, my dog goes too—and so does a mystery it seems. Choo is short for "ah-choo!" because she sneezes when she finds important clues. People are amazed that her sniffer has helped solve so many mysteries.

"Eva, try not to spill your water on the cake this

time," teased Bryce.

Don't remind me how clumsy I am, I thought. It's *so* embarrassing.

Dottie calls us the Tuesday Table #7 Club. Every Tuesday at 3:33 p.m. on the dot, Bryce, Donna, Cole, Nancy and I meet at The Topsy-Turvy Café. We always sit at table #7 and we always share a Caramel Apple Upside-Down Cake.

The Topsy-Turvy really *is* topsy-turvy, upside down and wacky. It looks like Wanda, the owner, was all mixed up when she decorated the place.

Dining tables hang upside down from the ceilings, and they're set with plates, teacups, teapots—even upside-down vases of flowers. Crooked windows tilt this way and that. The menu is silly, too (for example, Every Which Way Pasta, Backwards BBQ, Jumbled Juice Smoothies and Hodgepodge* Stew).

"Today it's my treat because I hit the jackpot," Dottie said as we all raised our forks. She slowly slipped her hand into the pocket of her green-and-purple polka-dotted apron and a big grin spread across her pretty face. "Well, hot-diggity-dog! Wait till you check out my genuine* treasure!"

All forks stopped in midair. Six pairs of eyes (including Choo's) went straight to her pocket.

"This is my lucky day," she said. "This morning I found a lucky penny in my tip jar!" She held up an old copper coin between her thumb and pointer finger.

It didn't look much like a treasure to me.

Donna crinkled her nose. "My Aunt Lillian collects coins. But *hers* are nice and shiny."

Nancy elbowed Donna and hissed, "Shhh! Mind your manners."

Otis, the café dishwasher, and Mr. Deebee, the baker who delivers the pies and cakes, gathered around as Dottie told us the whole fantastic story.

"A few weeks ago, I was hanging a poster advertising the coin show that starts tomorrow. Mr. Deebee said he'd been to last year's coin show and boy would he like to look through my tip jar. He told me that one of the coins might be worth a *fortune*.

"That got me thinking," Dottie continued. "I checked a book out of the library on coin collecting. It showed me exactly what makes some coins valuable.

I looked at each coin in my tip jar under a magnifying glass.

"And what do you know? I found this 1955 double die* Lincoln penny! It's worth about a thousand dollars!"

Out of the corner of my eye, I saw Mr. Deebee squint and scrunch his mouth over to one side. You'd think he might have been a little happier for Dottie.

"The U.S. Mint* made a mistake. The year '1955' and the words 'Liberty' and 'In God We Trust' are doubled*. That boo-boo is what makes the penny valuable."

"Wow! That's a great story. Can I take your photo for the newspaper?" I asked. I zoomed in on the penny that Dottie was proudly holding and snapped a picture.

We all wanted to hold the coin and take a closer look. Cole made a grab for it before anyone else had a chance. He put it right up to his eye. I couldn't wait to get my hands on it. He took his sweet time, then finally passed it to me.

"Thanks," I said.

"Once I sell this coin," Dottie said excitedly, "I can buy a train ticket to go visit my sister. I can't wait to—"

Just then the welcome bell on the café's front door jingled and someone shouted inside, "Come quick! The One-Wheel Wonder is almost here! Hurry!"

I had to get a photo of Captain Chris, The One-Wheel Wonder, for *The Scoop*. Dressed in a captain's hat and white uniform, he was setting a world record by riding a unicycle* while playing the banjo, all the way from the coast of California to Boston Harbor. We'd been waiting two months for him to pass through our town.

Every person in The Topsy-Turvy jostled* out the door to see and hear The One-Wheel Wonder.

I was the last to scramble from my chair. As I did, my hand caught the edge of the cake platter. The next few seconds seemed like they were in s-l-o-w m-o-t-i-o-n.

Ffffffffffflip…fffffffffffflop…ssssssssssplat! Now the Caramel Apple Upside-Down Cake was truly upside down, and all over the table, the floor, the chairs and me.

What a klutz. What a mess. What would I tell my friends?

As it was, they teased me constantly about having fumblefingers, chanting:

E-va, E-va,
A big dis-grace,
Knock-ing everything,
Out of place!

Chapter Two

MIX-UP AT THE TOPSY-TURVY

Do something, I thought—*and fast*. Quick as a wink, I scraped all the chunks that were once a cake into the garbage can.

I scooted into the kitchen and put the sticky dishes into a big sink full of hot sudsy water. I wrung out a dishrag and wiped up apples and sauce that had oozed all over table #7. Standing on a chair, I stashed the round tray on the bottom of the upside-down table, grabbed a broom and swept up hundreds of tiny crumbs.

Choo twitched her nose, sneezed and licked dripping caramel off my sneaker.

"Thanks for helping me clean, honey. I can always count on you." I started to rub her belly but noticed how messy my fingers were. "Let's go to the bathroom and wash up."

As I scrubbed, the welcome bell jingled. A paper towel

soaked in water got most of the sweet stuff off of my sneaker. The bell jingled again. *Uh-oh*, I thought, *everyone must be coming back inside.*

I peeked out the door and was surprised to see that the café was still empty except for Otis, who was bending over by table #7. He stood up, nodded to himself and smiled, then tucked his hand into his apron pocket.

Mr. Deebee's loud voice boomed from the kitchen. "I put nine Higgledy-Piggledy* Pies in the fridge."

Otis scurried through the swinging doors into the kitchen. Had he figured out what I'd done? Pies he liked. Kids he didn't. He'd just love to spill the beans and get me in trouble.

A second later, I heard the back door slam and Mr. Deebee's delivery van roar away.

I sat down in the empty café. *Whew!* No trace of the accident remained. The bell jingled again and all the customers filed back inside. Otis looked in unusually good spirits as he pushed the kitchen doors open and began sweeping the café floor.

"Eva, you missed The One-Wheel Wonder. What have you been doing?" Donna asked.

"More importantly," accused Bryce, "what did you do

with the cake?"

The first thing that popped into my head popped out of my mouth. "I-I-I-I ate it."

"You ATE it?!" gasped Nancy. "A whole cake? You chowed down that huge cake? Where are your manners?"

"I only got one bite," Donna whined. "Just one forkful."

"I was really hungry," I squeaked. "You wouldn't *believe* how hungry."

"You didn't leave any at all for us?" Mad faces stared from all directions.

Dottie clanged* the cash register drawer shut, gave her customers their change and strolled over to our table. "Are you done looking at the coin? I'd like to put it in my purse for safekeeping."

Everybody looked at me. "*You* had it last, Eva."

"I...um, I....don't..."

"Did you eat that, too?" Donna huffed.

I checked my pockets. I looked around wildly. I bit my lip. I thought I saw steam shooting out of Dottie's nose and ears.

I'd lost the coin.

Otis pointed his long finger at me. "She stole the penny! That little thief stole the coin!"

19

Chapter Three

GADZOOKS* & GOODY GUMDROPS

Telling fibs is like blowing bubbles. You can't stop at just one.

The scene at The Topsy-Turvy was terrible. I tried to explain that I didn't steal the penny. But let's face it, who would believe that? I was the last person to have the coin. Everyone but me was outside watching Captain Chris. It certainly looked like I was the thief.

The owner of the café, Wanda, asked everyone to please stop yelling and calm down. Wanda said the coin probably rolled off the table. At closing time, after all the customers had left, she'd search the place to find the penny.

"For now," Wanda told me, "go on home. When your phone rings tonight, it will be me telling you the coin was found hiding in some crack or corner."

I sure hoped so. But still…would my friends ever trust me again? Was steam still spouting from Dottie's head? I didn't dare look.

Close to tears, I scooped up Choo and ran to the parking lot. I hopped on Buzz, my hot-pink scooter, and Choo jumped into her matching sidecar*. I put Choo's little black biker jacket and pink goggles on her, adjusted our helmets and we started to zip home. I was innocent, so why did I feel like a robber making a getaway?

I felt sick.

My mom sensed something was wrong as soon as I walked through our front door. "What's the matter, Eva?"

"Not feeling so hot," I murmured, rubbing my tummy.

"Oh my, you'd better go right upstairs to your room and lie down."

I dragged my slumpy, droopy, tired body up the stairs, curled up on my bed and started to cry.

Loud bawling. Tears the size of water balloons. The works. It was hard to catch my breath. I pounded my fist into my fuzzy pillow. *I wish this day had never happened*, I thought.

In the history of the whole world, no one has ever felt sorrier for herself than I did for me right then.

My great big sobs were so noisy, it was amazing that I heard the phone ringing downstairs. *Thank goodness*, I thought, *Wanda must have found the penny.* I wiped my eyes. I suddenly felt better. Hopeful. Hungry.

Not two minutes later my bedroom door opened and my mom stepped in. *Gadzooks!* Her arms were folded across her chest and her lips were tightly pressed together.

"Well, I can see why your stomach hurts, Eva. Bryce's mother just phoned. Do you know what's more disappointing than you devouring* an entire cake?"

Here it comes, I thought. *The stolen penny.*

"Not sharing with your friends," she continued. "That's just not like you. And I cooked your favorite dinner, too—lasagna and garlic bread. Well, you'd better skip that. I'm sure you can't fit another thing in your stomach."

She took a deep breath. "Do you have anything to say for yourself?"

If I admitted the truth now, she'd call Bryce's mom. Bryce's mom would tell Bryce. Bryce would call all my friends. Then the teasing about me having butterfingers would be even worse. Believe it or not, it seemed easier to tell another fib.

"I'm really sorry," I said. And I *was* sorry, boy was I.

R-r-r-r-ring! My mom went downstairs to answer the phone.

It's Wanda, I hoped. *Goody gumdrops!* I was so

relieved, I decided I'd confess the little white lies.

I heard my mom climbing the stairs and a minute later she plunked herself down on my bed and sighed. "The manager from Perk Up just called. She's hopping* mad about your photos on the front page of *The Scoop*—and so are a lot of businesses in town."

R-r-r-r-ring! R-r-r-r-ring! R-r-r-r-ring!

I closed my eyes and hoped some more. *Pleeeeeeease let that be Wanda.*

She pushed herself up from my bed and padded downstairs again to answer the phone. Then with a clomp, clomp, clomp, clomp, clomp, clomp, clomp, she came back up the stairs. *What now*, I thought?

Her hands were on her hips. Her cheeks were bright red. She was slowly shaking her head.

"You have some explaining to do, Eva. What's become of Dottie's valuable coin?"

Dear Me!
Advice & Chitchat

Dear Me,

My town is so tiny, everybody knows everybody—and everybody else's beeswax, too. That's why the shocking upset this week at the local café spread like maple syrup on a hot pancake.

My goodness, what a fuss! A dear sweet girl, who we'll call "E" is smack-dab in the middle of it all.

Do you know, rumors are flying that she's lying, stealing and all kinds of nonsense? *Imagine.* Take it from me, she's no crook. I know her *personally.*

The problem is that she did tell a teeny-tiny fib. Then she told another fib to cover up the first one, which led to one more....

A mess I tell you. A real mess.

How can she get folks to understand this is a huge mistake? How can she clear her name?

Signed,

Concerned and Quite Worried

Dear Concerned and Quite Worried:

I have three words for "E": Fix the fibs!

"E" must tell the truth. *Ouch!* I know that's going to sting.

The sooner she gets that over with, the sooner she'll feel a whole lot better.

Two heads are better than one. Here's a thought: Ask the public to help find the actual robber.

She could use the money in her piggy bank to buy a huge billboard that says "Wanted: Coin Thief" and "Reward: Three packs of grape bubblegum for information leading to the arrest of the robber." Or hire an airplane to pull a giant banner across the sky.

Has "E" considered calling the FBI to look into the matter? They're pros with this type of crime.

Better yet, write to the President.

"E" can't change what's already been said and done. But she can change what she does next.

Get to the bottom of this mystery. Investigate. Gather clues. Get the help of a furry friend.

Keep me posted*. Good luck!

Chapter Four

LUCKY PENNY, MY FOOT!

"Ah-choo!" Choo's sneeze startled me awake. I lifted my head from my desk and rubbed my eyes. My watch read 6:36 p.m. The wonderful smell of lasagna and garlic bread baking filled my room.

Something was stuck to the side of my face. It was the bookmark I'd made at Camp Tuckaway. I guess I'd dozed off after writing my "Dear Me!" column.

The whole lousy day came to mind. Wanda hadn't found the rare coin. Everyone thought I polished off a whole cake. My name was mud* in town because of the article I'd written.

❧ ❧

After dinner, my mom and I had a heart-to-heart talk.

"I'm sorry I lied, Mom," I said, and then told her what had happened at the café.

She said there was nothing to be done about the cake. "But friends don't lie to each other. Find a good time to tell your friends the *real* story." She was right.

"Tell them that the chant about you being clumsy hurts your feelings. There's a good chance they'll stop.

"About the garbage article," she advised, "journalists must tell the news honestly. If you did that, then you did your job." She was right again.

"As for the missing coin," she said, "I believe you and I believe *in* you. However, you *were* the last person to have the penny and that means you're responsible for it. Either find the penny or find a way to pay Dottie for what it's worth." In my heart, I knew she was right about this, too.

How would it be possible to earn enough money to pay Dottie for the coin? I had just spent the last $1.59 from my summer lemonade stand on a glittery, new lime-green detective notebook.

I'd be 102 before I'd earn enough money to pay Dottie back. On Sunday, I'd be turning ten, so I supposed that I'd give her some of my birthday present money.

Unless, of course, the penny was found. If the coin wasn't anywhere to be found in The Topsy-Turvy, and if *I* didn't take it (which I didn't), then someone else surely did. But who?

Hmmmm. I looked up at Choo's official "Qualified Canine* Investigator" diploma from the Puppy Police Academy that was framed above my desk.

"Choo," I said, rubbing her belly, "what we have on our hands—and paws—is a mystery to solve!"

So we did what good investigators do: we jotted down a list of possible suspects* and clues in my detective notebook.

	The Mystery of the Vanishing Coin
○	SUSPECT #1: OTIS
	After the big Caramel Apple Upside-Down Cake cleanup, Otis was by table #7. He tucked his hand into his pocket. Was he smiling because he found the penny? MOTIVE*: Otis is always complaining about how he's a starving artist and broke* college student. Many coin dealers (people who buy and sell coins) will be at the coin show this week. Does he plan on selling the penny there?
○	ALSO: He doesn't seem that crazy about kids. That's weird.
○	SUSPECT #2: DONNA ☹
	I had the coin last—*or did I?* Everything happened so quickly. I can't remember if I set it down when we got up to see The One-Wheel Wonder. Donna was right next to me. Did she scoop it up on her way out of the café? (She's one of my best friends, so I can't imagine she'd do such a thing.)
○	MOTIVE: She needs a special present for her Aunt Lillian.
	ALSO: Aunt Lillian is a coin collector.

"Looks like we have two suspects, Choo," I said, petting the spot she likes right behind her velvety-soft ears.

Choo trotted over to her bell that hangs on my doorknob. Whenever she wants to go outside, she gives it one quick jingle to let me know.

"Ah-choo!" Then she jingled the bell once. Jingled the bell again.

Two jingles. I'd heard that sound earlier. We were in the bathroom at The Topsy-Turvy and the welcome bell jingled once. A minute later, it jingled a second time. When we came out of the bathroom, Otis was the only person there. Someone else must have come inside, too.

"Who else was in the café, Choo?" I asked.

Choo licked her chops like she does when she thinks of something good to eat.

"Of course. The nine pies. You smart sleuth*." We added a third suspect to the list.

The Mystery of the Vanishing Coin

SUSPECT #3: MR. DEEBEE

We heard Mr. Deebee's voice in the kitchen. He might have been the first person to come inside, seen the coin and snatched it. While he was unloading the Higgledy-Piggledy Pies from the truck, Otis might have entered the café.

MOTIVE: It was Mr. Deebee's idea in the first place to look through the tip jar for a valuable coin. Was he so mad that Dottie found the coin—instead of him—that he stole it?

ALSO: What was his rush to leave the café? Was he afraid of getting caught?

I drummed my fingers on the desk. I fiddled with a shiny old-fashioned key that dangled from my necklace. *That's it*, I thought. "It's time for some detective work, Choo. Let's see what costumes we have to begin our undercover* investigation."

I glanced at the fancy pink-and-cream trunk at the foot of my bed.

I removed my necklace, put the key in the trunk's lock and turned it one full circle. Click. I lifted the lid.

"Aaaaaahhhhhhhh!" I scrambled away and gasped in horror. My heart was racing so fast I'm surprised it didn't beat me out the bedroom door.

Chapter Five

EYE SPY A GOOD DISGUISE*

"Are you OK, Eva?!" My mom came bounding up the stairs.

I gulped as she put her arm around my shoulders and gently led me back into the bedroom. Too frightened to speak, I pointed to a large-as-life tiger head glaring up at me from the big trunk.

"Oh, I see you found the roaring tiger costume." She picked up the head and put it on. "Don't these fangs look real?"

Phew! Up close, it was obvious it was totally fake—fake fur, eyes and teeth.

"Rraaaarrrhhh!" she roared. "I found it at a yard sale and thought it might come in handy for your undercover detective work. You gave me your other key so I put this costume in your disguise trunk. Guess it fooled you, huh?"

She giggled all the way down the hallway.

I knelt back down beside the trunk. To solve mysteries, I often have to go incognito (that means changing what I really look like so people won't recognize me).

This trunk holds all the disguises I've ever used.

I pulled out the big blue wings and antennae that Choo and I wore to investigate The Mystery of the Haunted Hotel. Someone was spooking the guests and the owners were losing business. As I slipped into the fairy costume, I smiled thinking about how we solved the case the night of the hotel's Halloween party.

"Remember solving The Secret at Abracadabra Academy, Choo?" I showed her the magician's top hat, long black cape and wand we used. "To find the pirate's treasure map that disappeared, we enrolled as students in a magic school, followed the clues and—alakazam! There it was rolled up inside Myra the Magician's wand. And you figured out that her assistant was in on the vanishing act, too."

Choo got up from her cushy pink bed that's built into my desk, gave a big stretch, yawned and peeked over the edge of the trunk. She nudged a black mustache with long, curling ends, white chef's jacket and puffy white hat.

"Ah, yes, The Riddle in the Kitchen," I teased. "That's your favorite kind of detective work—fun *and* delicious."

"Ah-choo!"

"What are you thinking, Choo?" I wondered aloud. "Let's see…chef, cook, baker…suspect #3 is a baker… ah-ha! Use the disguise to see if the baker stole the coin. Very clever." Choo wagged her tail and smiled.

"I have a plan. I'll pick you up on Buzz tomorrow afternoon. We just might catch the thief."

Dear Me!
Advice & chitchat

Dear Me,

"E's" article sure has ruffled feathers in this town.

Yes, she wrote the article. Yes, she took the photos on the front page of *The Scoop*. But local businesses are partly to blame for the trash. Their names are printed all over the cups and wrappers that litter the streets.

Customers could bring their water bottles, cups and containers home to recycle them. But it would be easier for people to recycle a lot of that trash if there were recycling bins beside the garbage cans.

Ms. Werner, who is the head of the school newspaper and also "E's" English teacher, thinks the big hoo-ha* might be a good thing.

Here's why: when a problem hits the news, people start talking. Talk can lead to ideas. Ideas can lead to change.

The school's recycling club, called The Green Team, asked Ms. Werner if the paper would do an article next month called "Trash Talk: Where Are All The Recycling Bins?"

She's all for it and thinks "E" is just the person to write the story.

"E's" not so sure. She wants to be a good reporter and "tell it like it is." But she also wants people to like her.

She's in a pickle*.

If writing the recycling article is the right thing to do, why does it feel so wrong?

Signed,
Frowning in Whistle Creek

Dear Frowning in Whistle Creek:

I have three words for "E":
Do something positive!

It's time to stop feeling sorry for herself and start taking action.

This is no pickle she's in. It's the perfect chance to get things changed— for the better.

Right now she has the town's attention. The time is right to write that article.

Don't just report the problems, suggest solutions.

Remember what Ms. Werner says good journalists* must always do: state the facts, but don't jump to conclusions*.

Keep me posted. Good luck!

Chapter Six
EAT YOUR HEART OUT

As I trudged along the sidewalk the next morning on the way to school, I braced myself for facing my friends. Would they still talk to me?

Surprisingly, they were as sweet as pie. Even nicer than usual. But as the old saying goes, if something seems too good to be true, it usually is.

At lunchtime, the cafeteria was decorated for the Five-a-Day Festival. The school nurses held the event each year to remind students to eat five servings of fruits and vegetables every day. There are games about eating healthfully, prizes and yummy samples, too (it's heaven for a vegetarian* like me).

This day is going much better than expected, I told myself. I heard my name coming from the loudspeaker.

"Our first contestant* for the Watermelon Eating Contest is Eva," the principal announced. "She'll be hard to beat, folks. A little birdie told me she ate a whole cake yesterday!"

My friends had been up to no good all along. All except for Nancy, that is. She stuck her bottom lip out and made a sad face to let me know she felt sorry for me.

"We put your name on the contest list this morning," Donna said a little too sweetly.

"We *know* you can do it," chimed in Cole.

Bryce was all too pleased to end with the zinger, "You'll *steal* the show."

On my way up to the contest table, I heard a new twist on the old chant:

E-va, E-va,

A big dis-grace,

Stuff-ing everything,

In her face!

⋘ ⋙

That morning my mom had reminded me that Wanda wanted me to stop by The Topsy-Turvy after school. When I got there I asked one of the waitresses if I could speak with Wanda.

"Sit tight, hon," she said, "Wanda's on the phone so it will be a few minutes."

I sat at table #7 and thought about how The Green Team's president, Wendie, had stopped by my locker after lunch.

"Did you know that the average American creates over four pounds of trash a day?" Wendie asked. "Some of that trash could be recycled and used to make other things. Maybe the article you're writing will get businesses to put out recycling bins for their customers."

I had mixed feelings. The article might stir up a whole pot of trouble. At the same time, I was starting to get excited. This was my chance to help save the planet.

She continued, "If The Green Team helps out at the coin show's concession* stand, the catering chef said we can sell our 'Save The Planet' reusable fabric grocery bags and travel mugs. We'll use the money we make to buy recycling bins for the gym. Want to help?"

I was happy she asked. The concession stand was located in the hallway, right outside the doors of the coin show. It was the perfect spot to spy on suspects. I told her I'd be there before 5:00 p.m. when the show opened.

My thoughts were interrupted when a dish clattered to the floor. Otis picked it up, wiped his hands on his polka-dotted apron, and then glanced my way. I shot him a look. Some nerve he had, accusing me of stealing Dottie's coin.

I leafed through my geography book, then heard Wanda coming through the swinging doors. I used the 2nd place ribbon I'd won in the Watermelon Eating Contest as a bookmark for Chapter 3.

"Glad you dropped by," said Wanda, as she pulled up a chair and sat down.

Oh boy, I thought, *here comes the lecture on what a disappointment I am.*

"Your mom said that you intend to pay Dottie for the value of the missing coin. I have an idea that will help you and me, too."

She went on to explain that The Topsy-Turvy had opened 50 years ago. To celebrate their anniversary, they were inviting everyone in Whistle Creek to a Wonderfully Wacky Wingding* on Sunday.

"It's going to be huge! But Otis will be on vacation that week, so we could really use your help washing dishes the day of the party. Maybe you could use the money you earn to help pay Dottie for the coin. How do you feel about that?"

I glanced away. *I feel it's unfair to have to pay for something I didn't steal*, I thought.

My gaze met Wanda's. She was being so kind, making it seem like I'd be doing her a big favor if I helped out at the celebration. In truth, she was doing *me* a favor. "Thanks, Wanda. I always wash the dinner dishes, so I'm a pro."

"Good, then you're hired!" She smiled and we shook on it. "Come by on Friday before Otis leaves for Fifties Night. He'll show you around the kitchen so you'll know where to put the dishes after they're washed."

"Fifties Night?" I asked.

"Every weekend the dance studio teaches a different kind of dance lesson. Last week it was Salsa* Night and the week before that it was Hip-Hop* Night. This Friday it's a sock hop. Everyone dresses in clothing that was popular in the 1950s and learns dances from that time."

She handed me a green-and-purple polka-dotted apron, which is The Topsy-Turvy uniform.

On the way out the door, I picked up a plastic fork that had toppled from the heaping pile in the trash can. I carefully set it on top of water bottles, cans, ice cream cups and paper napkins, hoping the whole stack wouldn't fall over.

What they need is a recycling bin, I thought.

Maybe I could suggest to Wanda that they get one. Then again, maybe I should just zip my lip. Hadn't I rocked* the boat enough?

Wait a minute! When I wrote the story for *The Scoop* about businesses that were not doing their part to recycle, would I have to mention The Topsy-Turvy?

How could I do that to Wanda after all she'd done for me?

Chapter Seven
HIDE & GO SEEK

Mr. Deebee is known for his Higgledy-Piggledy Pies and Caramel Apple Upside-Down Cakes. But his most famous creation by far is his Buried Treasure Cake. It's baked only once a year, especially for the coin show.

It's called a Buried Treasure Cake because a coin wrapped in foil is hidden inside. The person who gets the slice with the coin is supposed to have good luck for a whole year.

Everyone wants the one-and-only Buried Treasure Cake, but here's the catch—you *can't* buy it. You have to win it in the coin show raffle. The concession stand sells tickets for $1 each or ten tickets for $5. All the money goes to the Whistle Creek Animal Shelter. (That's where I adopted my best friend Choo.)

If my hunch* was correct, Mr. Deebee would deliver

the Buried Treasure Cake right before the show began. Then he'd make a beeline* for the booths and try to sell Dottie's penny to one of the dealers.

My watch read 4:34 p.m. I pulled into a parking space and Choo and I hopped off Buzz. She sniffed around while I removed the chef's uniform and curling mustache from my hot-pink backpack and put it on.

Wendie and a few kids from the recycling club were already at the concession stand. At first they didn't recognize me in my disguise, so I figured Mr. Deebee wouldn't either. When they heard my voice, they joked, "Well, if it isn't Eva the gourmet*!"

"Hey, chef," Wendie teased me, "can you please find the box of fliers about recycling?"

Crouching down to look under the table, I heard a familiar voice behind me.

"No no no!" the man boomed. "This Buried Treasure Cake must be displayed right here where everyone can see it when they enter and exit. Let me talk to the chef. He'll get this straightened out!"

My heart stopped. Uh-oh. S-l-o-w-l-y I rose and began to turn around.

46

A gentle voice came from a round man in a white chef's coat and red neckerchief, wearing a hat just like mine. "Mr. Deebee, by all means, put your beautiful cake right here." The catering chef cleared room on the table.

"That's more like it!" Mr. Deebee beamed as he set the chocolate cake down ever so carefully. He entered the show and zigzagged through the crowd.

"Nice outfit," the chef said to me with a little wink.

Bryce was the first person to come to the concession

stand. "I'd like to buy one Buried Treasure Cake raffle ticket, please."

"But," I said, still keeping my sights on Mr. Deebee, "buying ten is a better deal and gives you more chances to win." Wendie had told me to say this to raise more money.

"Nope," he said. "One is plenty lucky." I shrugged, took his dollar and gave him a ticket.

I saw Mr. Deebee stop at the King's Coins booth. He spoke with the dealer and reached into his pocket. *There he goes*, I thought, *he's going to show Dottie's 1955 double die penny to the man and see how much he can get for it.*

A group of people wandered into the booth and blocked my view of Mr. Deebee.

"Be back in a sec," I said to Wendie as I rushed out of the concession stand. By the time I made my way through the crowd to the front of King's Coins, Mr. Deebee was long gone.

"I'd like to ask you about a 1955 double die Lincoln penny," I told Mr. King, the dealer.

"Funny thing," Mr. King replied, "just a few minutes

48

ago, a fellow asked me if I'd be interested in buying that particular penny. Excuse me for a moment though, because there are a few people ahead of you in line."

Cole stepped up to the concession stand. "May I please have an apple cider?" A confused look came over his face. "Oh, Eva, it's *you*. When did you grow a mustache?"

He unzipped his blue backpack, pulled out a dollar bill and set the backpack on the floor.

"Would you like me to put it in a reusable travel mug for just $1 more?" I asked him. That was another sales pitch* Wendie had taught me.

He shook his head no and waited while I poured his drink.

"OK then, don't forget to put your empty paper cup in the recycling bin," I reminded him. That's what Wendie told me to say if people were too cheap to fork over the cash for a mug.

"Ah-choo!" I looked down at Choo, who was

nosing around inside Cole's backpack. She tossed her head from one side to the other then pulled out a crumpled up piece of paper.

Choo must want me to recycle that, I thought, as I picked up the scrap of paper. One of Cole's friends called to him, he gave me a kind-of sort-of wave goodbye and walked away.

Just before I dropped the paper into the recycling bin, one word caught my attention.

"Lincoln." How odd. Lincoln? As in Abraham Lincoln, the president whose face is on pennies? I smoothed the paper out on the table. It read:

Return Lincoln tomorrow—or pay the price!

Chapter Eight

HOT ON THE TRAIL

On Thursday, before school, I added to the detective notebook:

	The Mystery of the Vanishing Coin
○	NEW CLUE ABOUT SUSPECT #3: MR. DEEBEE
	He asked the dealer at King's Coins if he would be interested in buying a 1955 double die Lincoln penny. Does he have one to sell?
	SUSPECT #4: COLE ☹
○	What was the meaning of the note in Cole's backpack? Was it a threat? Was he going to slip it into my locker? (He's one of my best friends, so I can't believe he'd do that.) Or was it a reminder to himself to bring the stolen penny back to The Topsy-Turvy and drop it on the floor. Once it was found, everyone would think it had been lost the whole time.
	MOTIVE: Remember how he grabbed the penny when Dottie first showed it to us? He was unusually interested in that coin.
	ALSO: He is still pretty ticked off at me for eating the cake. Maybe he just
○	wanted to see me squirm*.

"Hey, chef," Wendie whispered from her desk. "Big news. On Saturday, The Green Team is holding a demonstration."

"What's a demonstration?" I asked.

"It's a public meeting where people show they don't agree with something that's happening. In this case, we want to show businesses in town that we don't agree with all the garbage they're creating.

"You're in, right? Come and hold signs with us and you'll get the inside story for the article you're writing."

"Sounds like a good idea," I agreed.

She gave me a high-five. "Great. See you at 10:00 a.m. right across the street from The Topsy-Turvy."

Oh no! Why had I said yes?

The garbage problem isn't the only thing that stinks around here, I thought. It stunk that Wanda's feelings might be hurt when she saw me demonstrating across the street. Would she think I was a backstabber*?

Why had I been such a scaredy-cat to talk to her about getting a recycling bin for the café?

Our teacher clapped her hands to get everyone's attention. "All right class, listen up. Today we're discussing fables. A fable is a story that teaches a lesson about right and wrong or good and bad.

"We'll begin with the story, *The Boy Who Cried Wolf*." She scanned the room. Her eyeballs locked in on mine. Was

she trying to say something to me?

"Does anyone know what it's about?"

Keith, whose mom owns Perk Up Coffee Shop, shot his hand up in the air, "It's about how people in a town get furious with a know-it-all kid," he said, looking over one shoulder at me, "and wish the kid would just keep her silly thoughts to herself."

Another kid raised her hand and said the story is about how boring it is to watch a flock of sheep all day.

When the teacher called on me, I said, "It's about how nobody can trust a liar, even when the liar is telling the truth."

53

"You should know," Bryce muttered*.

☙ ❧

"Forget about the cake," Nancy said to me at lunch. "Everybody makes a mistake once in awhile. And I know you didn't take Dottie's penny." She was trying to make me feel better because Cole, Bryce and Donna were hardly speaking to me. *Come on people, it was just a cake.*

I tried to patch things up with Donna. "What time do you want to go to the mall on Saturday afternoon?"

She avoided looking at me and inspected the fingernails on her right hand. "I don't have to go to the mall anymore."

I was shocked. She'd been bugging me for two weeks to go shopping. "What about your Aunt Lillian's gift?"

She chipped nail polish off her thumbnail. "Never mind. I already found one."

"Y-y-y-you did? Wh-what is it?" I stammered.

"It's a—it's a—*perfect* present." Hastily she added, "And she's going to *love* it."

I see. So. She wasn't going to tell me. It sounded more than a little suspicious*.

54

Dear Me!
Advice & chitchat

Dear Me,

The hullabaloo* continues!

Goodness gracious, everyone is still all riled up about the coin, the cake and the article on garbage.

After reading the book Wendie gave her on what garbage is doing to the earth, "E" was shocked. Did you know...

...that America makes more trash than any country on the planet?

....that a can takes 100 to 500 years to rot?

...that in just one year, Americans used so many plastic bottles, the empty bottles would fill big truck trailers lined up from Boston, Massachusetts to Los Angeles, California?

...that plastic bags and plastic trash kill up to one million sea creatures every year?

...that if each person in the U.S. recycled their newspapers just one day a week, 36 million trees would be saved?

People should know this stuff!

"E's" problems are bound to get worse if she demonstrates with The Green Team on Saturday.

The question is: does she have the guts to stand out there?

Will the crew at The Topsy-Turvy be mad?

Will she get kicked out of the Tuesday Table #7 Club?

Will she ever get to taste Caramel Apple Upside-Down Cake again?

Signed,

All Worked Up

Dear All Worked Up,

I have three words for "E":
Follow your heart!

Abraham Lincoln said, "Be sure you put your feet in the right place, then stand firm."

I think that means do what you believe in and don't be wishy-washy. If "E" believes in protecting the earth, she should stand proudly at the demonstration and get the word out.

Keep me posted. Good luck!

Chapter Nine

REDUCE, REUSE, REPAIR & RECYCLE

When I went to The Topsy-Turvy after school on Friday to get the kitchen tour, Otis was in a big rush. He quickly pointed out how to stack the dishes and where the pans and trays were kept.

He checked his watch. "No questions, right?"

A couple of questions ran through my mind: *Did you steal Dottie's coin? Are you going to Fifties Night or secretly going to the coin show instead?*

"Now that you mention it—" I started.

Otis interrupted me, "Look, I have to pick up my date in an hour and I still have to change, so…seeeeeee yaaaa."

Sounded like a pretty sorry excuse to me. Who in the world would date Otis?

Anyway, what he didn't know was that I was in a

hurry, too—to see where he was *really* going.

I jogged home to get the outfit that my mom used to wear. Back when she was a student, her school had a sock hop every year. I changed into her pink poodle skirt, striped T-shirt, pink scarf and black-and-white saddle shoes. Choo couldn't have looked any cuter in her poodle disguise, with a pink scarf and poodle earmuffs and slippers.

My mom was still at work, so I left a note on the kitchen counter that I'd be home at 5:30 p.m. Choo and I jumped on Buzz, buckled up and arrived at The Dance Studio a few minutes later.

Dressed in my disguise, I blended right in with the other dancers in fifties costumes. I searched the crowd. *Surprise, surprise.* Otis was there after all. I didn't see his date. I knew it.

It was possible that he might leave early and go to the coin show. He could sell that 1955 penny quickly and pay for his vacation.

I saw my favorite summer camp counselor and we started yackety-yacking. Her stories were so funny I completely forgot I was on the job as a detective.

Next thing I knew, I sensed a tall person on my right staring at me.

"What are *you* doing here?" Otis demanded. He was wearing rolled-up jeans, a blue jacket with white sleeves and a big letter on it, a white T-shirt, white socks and penny loafers.

My camp counselor slipped her hand in his. *She* was his date?!

I couldn't help myself. Another fib slipped out. "Well, you know, uh, I heard dancing is good for your brain. So here I am, ready to rock-and-roll and exercise my mental muscles."

"No kidding." He scowled. "Is Choo planning on learning the jitterbug*, too?"

Choo looked up at me with her big eyes, as if to say, "He's on to us, and he won't risk going to the coin show now."

I'd blown it. It wasn't just suspects that were piling up. The lies were, too.

✤ ✤

After dinner, there were no dishes to wash because my mom had brought home take-out burritos. All I had to do was clear the table.

As I started to throw away the trash, Choo twitched her nose and sneezed.

"Gee, Choo, you're right. All this garbage came from just one meal."

Little plastic salsa packages, styrofoam containers, tortilla chip bags, plastic bags, paper salt and pepper packets, plastic straws with paper wrappers, plastic forks, plastic juice bottles, plastic knives, paper napkins, plastic spoons....

What we need is a recycling bin, I thought.

I knew right then I had to DO something, starting that very minute. I asked my mom if we could get a recycling bin that weekend and she agreed.

I went to my bedroom, turned on the radio and got out my markers. I spent the rest of the night coloring a poster for the demonstration the next day.

REDUCE

Only buy stuff you really need.

REUSE

Have a yard sale! Your trash is someone else's treasure.

REPAIR

If it's broken, try to fix it before you toss it.

RECYCLE

Glass, cans, paper, cardboard and plastic

Butterflies fluttered in my stomach thinking about the demonstration.

Just before I slipped into bed, I got out my detective notebook and jotted down the events at the sock hop. There was a knock and my bedroom door opened.

"Eva, do you—" my mom stopped in the middle of her sentence. "That's a new notebook, isn't it? Where did you get the money to buy it?"

Why was she asking? "I used my money from last summer's lemonade stand."

"Oh." She stood there a moment, as if puzzled.

That was pretty much the end of the conversation. The look on her face was so strange. She didn't think that I stole Dottie's coin, sold it for cash and bought a new detective notebook, did she? *Of course not*, I thought. *Don't be silly*. Still, it left me feeling blue.

I put the finishing touches on my poster and sat back to look at it. "What do you think, Choo?"

She was lying down with her head resting on my camera bag, looking serious. "Ah-choo!"

I picked up the camera bag. Empty. Where was my camera? Let me think…I used it on Tuesday at The Topsy-Turvy to take Dottie's picture. Come to think of it, I couldn't remember seeing it since.

Oh no. It had taken me so long to save up the money to buy my new camera.

Wanda or Otis would have given it back to me if they had found it. Now two valuable items were missing from The Topsy-Turvy in one day. Was it the work of the same thief?

❦ ❧

When Choo and I got to the demonstration on Saturday morning, fifteen or twenty kids from The Green Team were already out on the sidewalk holding

signs. Teachers and parents were there, too.

"What's with the granny getup?" asked one of the kids. He was commenting about the little old lady disguise I was wearing—an old-fashioned floral dress, knit shawl, wire-rim glasses, head scarf, brown purse and cane. A couple of the girls oohed and aahed over Choo, who was adorable in an outfit that matched mine.

I didn't want to admit that I was hoping Wanda and the crew at The Topsy-Turvy wouldn't recognize me with The Green Team. If they did, my dishwashing job would end before it even began.

I took notes for the newspaper article, then interviewed recycling club members and people walking by. My mom had lent me her camera and I got some good photos of the signs.

Hundreds of cars drove past us. Some cars gave a short HONK-HONK to let us know they thought recycling was a good idea. A few people gave us dirty looks. Others gave us the thumbs-up or smiled.

I overheard one of the kids whispering to another, "I guess The Topsy-Turvy would rather close for the day than have their customers coming in asking why they don't recycle."

"Yeah," said her friend. "Maybe they found out that a reporter would be on the scene." She wagged her pointer finger at me. "They even covered the inside of their windows with brown paper so you can't see inside."

I couldn't believe my ears. The Topsy-Turvy was never closed on Saturday. Dottie told me it was always her best day for tips.

Dottie had lost her valuable coin and now she'd missed out on her biggest tips of the week.

I felt doubly terrible.

Choo can always tell when I'm down in the dumps. She rubbed up against my leg as if to say, "Hang in there. It will be OK." I knelt down and gave her a kiss on the top of her head. What a good friend.

Choo twitched her nose. "Ah-choo!" It was clear what she was trying to tell me. Litter had spilled from the garbage can behind her. She was standing on what looked like an upside-down flier.

"I know, Choo. The Green Team did the right thing today getting people to think about recycling. But doing the right thing isn't always the easiest thing."

I was more determined than ever to get to the bottom of this mystery.

We took off our disguises, left Buzz in the parking lot and walked over to the coin show. It was possible we'd get more information from Mr. King—or better yet, we'd see one of our suspects trying to sell the penny.

A loud noise that hurt my ears came over the loudspeaker. The DJ from the local radio station, WHHR-FM 101.3, announced, "Attention folks, last chance to buy your raffle tickets for the Buried Treasure Cake. The winner will be announced at 3:30 p.m."

"My oh my. Who do we have here?" I said to Choo. "If it isn't Cole, talking to one of the coin dealers."

Did this visit have something to do with the note Choo had found in Cole's backpack? Maybe he had decided to sell the Lincoln penny instead of returning it.

Quickly, I pulled a red baseball cap and sunglasses out of my backpack. This disguise works in almost any situation. I stayed far behind Cole so he wouldn't notice me.

What he did next surprised me. He pulled what looked like a coin from his pocket. Right out in the open. How bold!

The dealer examined it under a magnifier* and nodded his head. He and Cole spoke for a few minutes.

I couldn't help staring as the dealer counted out one, two, three, four, five, six, seven, eight, nine, ten bills in Cole's hand. Were they $100 bills? That adds up to $1,000. Isn't that what Dottie said her 1955 double die Lincoln penny might be worth?

Caught in the act!

Chapter Ten

YOU WIN SOME, YOU LOSE SOME

Had Cole let me take the blame for stealing the coin this whole time? I was fuming.

Choo dashed with me to the booth, but Cole was too quick for us. He'd taken the cash and hightailed* it out of there.

"Excuse me," I gasped to the dealer. I was out of breath from running. "Did you just buy a 1955 double die Lincoln penny from a no-good kid coin-crook a minute ago?"

He clenched his teeth. "That would make me part of a crime. I don't like what you are accusing me of doing."

Even though I said sorry twenty times, the dealer crossed his arms, turned his head, put his nose in the air and refused to speak another word to me.

At 3:30 p.m. the loudspeaker crackled and made an earsplitting sound. The DJ announced, "Our thanks again to Mr. Deebee, who donated the Buried Treasure Cake. Drum roll, please. We have a winner. Bryce takes the cake!"

Everybody in the place could hear his excited whoop.

On our walk back to the parking lot to get Buzz, Choo stopped and sniffed around by the overflowing trash can again. "Ah-choo!"

She sat down on the upside-down flier and pawed at it until she turned up one corner. The writing on the other side made me curious: "*new* recycling program." Choo stepped aside so I could pick up the paper. It read:

We're closed on Saturday while we prepare
for our 50th anniversary party.
Everyone is invited to The Topsy-Turvy Café's
WONDERFULLY WACKY WINGDING
on Sunday, noon to two o'clock.
Check out the big improvements when we reopen:
• *new* menu • *new* music stage • *new* recycling program

Wanda must have put this sign on the café's front door in the morning and it had blown off. Choo had tried to show it to me earlier.

The whole time The Green Team was outside demonstrating, the Topsy-Turvy staff was inside getting ready for the party—and putting out their new recycling bins. *That's* why the windows were covered with brown paper. They wanted their new and improved look to be a surprise.

If only I had talked to Wanda about it, I wouldn't have been worrying all this time. I should have done what good journalists do: get the facts instead of jumping to conclusions.

I let out a sigh of relief.

That night, I slipped into my cozy pink-and-white paw-print pajamas and flopped onto my bed. I jotted down the new clues while they were fresh in my mind. I fluffed up my fuzzy pillows behind my back and began to write:

The Mystery of the Vanishing Coin

NEW CLUE ABOUT SUSPECT #1: OTIS
Wanda said Otis was going on vacation. That's strange considering he's always complaining about being a starving artist and broke college student. Did he sell the coin on Saturday to get money to pay for a fabulous vacation like sailing around the world? Or traveling to Italy and eating all the lasagna and garlic bread he wants? (I would go to a water park seven days in a row, but that's just me.)

NEW CLUE ABOUT SUSPECT #2: DONNA ☹
Suddenly Donna finds the perfect present for her Aunt Lillian, the coin collector, and she won't tell me what it is. What's the big secret?

NEW CLUE ABOUT SUSPECT #4: COLE ☹
Cole sold a coin at the show. Was it Dottie's penny? The dealer paid him in cash. How much? $1,000?

PLUS: MY CAMERA IS MISSING!
It disappeared at just about the same time the coin vanished.

There were four suspects in all, but I didn't have a clue which one was to blame for stealing the penny. Actually, I had lots of clues. Maybe too many.

I switched off the light on my nightstand. Choo

curled up beside me, but neither of us could get to sleep. Music always relaxes me, so I tuned the radio to WHHR-FM 101.3. One of my favorite songs was just ending and faded into the newscaster's voice.

"Tomorrow is The Topsy-Turvy Café's 50th anniversary party. Not only is the café asking everyone in Whistle Creek to help them celebrate, they're also asking the public to help them solve a very baffling riddle—" I covered my ears.

Were they telling the whole dreadful stolen coin story? Would my name be on the radio?

Wait a minute. Maybe I'd drifted off to sleep and had a bad dream.

As I took one hand off my ear and reached over to click the radio's "off" button, the newscaster's voice was loud and clear, "…and it's worth a whopping $1,000!"

It wasn't a bad dream. It was a nightmare. And it was real.

I had a feeling that Sunday was going to be a birthday I'd never forget.

Chapter Eleven

UP TO HER EYES IN
HIGGLEDY-PIGGLEDY PIES

I was up to my elbows in suds when Wanda rushed into the kitchen. "You're doing a great job washing dishes, Eva. We're using them as fast as you clean them. I think half of Whistle Creek is here already!"

"Thanks. I meant to ask you where the forks and knives go," I said. "I don't remember Otis telling me that."

"That's because they're brand new—no more plastic silverware to throw away. Not only is The Topsy-Turvy recycling more, we're trying to reduce trash." She pointed to a drawer and added, "Put the forks and knives here. Then take a break and come join the party."

The truth is that I didn't want to. After hearing last night's radio announcement, I figured everyone in town knew I was the main suspect for stealing the rare coin.

Choo was acting a little odd. She kept licking my sneaker.

"Hey, silly, are you hungry?" The last time she licked my sneaker it was dripping with sticky, sweet caramel.

I knew that I had to face the crowd sooner or later, so I finished the silverware and pushed open the kitchen's swinging doors. The Topsy-Turvy was full of laughter, music and people having fun.

Cole was the only person who didn't seem to be having a good time. He appeared to be hiding beside the new music stage.

"Psst! Hey, Eva," he whispered. "Do you have that baseball cap and sunglasses with you?"

"Yes, why?"

"Can I borrow it? I don't want Mr. Chester to recognize me."

"Why don't you want the school librarian to recognize you?"

"Mr. Chester has been on my case every day because I keep forgetting to return a book about Abraham Lincoln. I even wrote myself a reminder note—but I lost it. It's way overdue, and now I have to pay the price—a *big* fine!"

"Um, Cole, that's a long story I should probably tell you," I began.

"Eva," interrupted Dottie, "I'm up to my eyes in Higgledy-Piggledy Pies, but I've run out of round trays to serve them on. Can you find some?"

"Sure thing," I said. Choo and I went into the kitchen.

Otis was there, dressed in his apron and was drying a pot. "What are you looking for?"

"Aren't you supposed to be on vacation?" I asked.

"The camping trip? Oh, my car broke down. Didn't have the cash to get it fixed." Otis shrugged. "I didn't want to miss this party anyway. After all, my new sculpture is in the café."

I must have looked puzzled.

He laughed. "OK, it's actually the new recycling bin, but it's art, too. It's called 'Tuesday Table #7' and it's covered entirely with the bottle caps I collected from table #7 after you guys left every week.

"I guess you might say that you and your friends inspired* my art. In fact, I found the last cap I needed under your table on Tuesday. Just in the nick of time."

Dottie barged through the doors. "Any luck finding trays, Eva? We're serving the pies right after the winner of the Wonderfully Wacky Wingding Riddle is announced."

"Huh? The Wonderfully Wacky Wingding Riddle?" I asked.

"You didn't hear about the contest on the radio last night?" Dottie asked. "Everybody takes a guess about how many berries it takes to make a Higgledy-Piggledy Pie. The winner gets a free Higgledy-Piggledy Pie every month for the rest of their life. The prize is easily worth a thousand dollars."

"You look for trays inside the café," Otis said to me, "while I search the kitchen."

Choo and I checked over and under the counter, then started at table #1 and made our way around the room to table #7.

"We'll help you," said Bryce, Nancy, Donna and Cole.

Choo was licking my sneaker again. I remembered the caramel mess I'd made the day the coin disappeared.

"Ah-choo!" Choo looked up at me. Or was she

76

looking at something *behind and above* me?

I turned, gazed up and spotted a round tray on the bottom of the upside-down table. "Good work, Choo."

"Choo found a tray for you, Dottie!" I hollered. Then I saw *IT*.

"Oh my goodness," cried Nancy.

"Do you see what I see?" Bryce asked.

Dottie's old copper coin was stuck to the bottom of the tray with a glob of caramel. I balanced on a chair and reached for the tray.

Right on top of the tray was my new camera.
"I hit the jackpot—again!" exclaimed Dottie.
I scooped up Choo. *Me too*, I thought.

Chapter Twelve
HAPPY BIRTHDAY TO ME

Those weren't the only surprises at The Topsy-Turvy that day.

While the Tuesday Table #7 Club helped sweep, wipe and wash up after the party, I was in the kitchen drying dishes with Otis.

Wanda came in. "Eva, may I please have a word with you in the café?" She sounded serious.

Here it comes, I thought, *she's going to tell me how disappointed she is that I didn't talk to her about recycling before we had the demonstration.*

I followed her into the café and saw an orangish glow coming from table #7.

"SURPRISE!"

All my friends, my mom, Dottie and Mr. Deebee were gathered around the table singing, "Happy

Birthday to you, happy birthday to you, happy birthday dear Eva, happy birthday to you!"

I couldn't believe what I was seeing. On the table was the one and only Buried Treasure Cake flickering with eleven candles (one for each year of my life, plus one for good luck).

Bryce grinned. "You sold me the winning ticket! You deserve it."

"As long as you don't snarf up the whole thing," joked Cole.

I made a wish and blew out the candles. Written on the cake in blue icing were these words:

E-va, E-va,
she's an ace,
mysteries get solved
when she's on the case!

We cut the cake so everyone could share it.

Otis coughed and sputtered. "Ayam nowt bwoek aweemoe," he mumbled with a mouth full of cake.

"Where are your manners?" Nancy scolded.

"I *said*," Otis declared, "I'm not broke anymore!" He pulled a tinfoil package from his slice of cake and unwrapped a shiny coin.

We all cracked up laughing.

Cake was eaten, party stories were told and quite a few of my questions were answered.

Mr. Deebee gave Dottie a business card from King's Coins. "I asked Mr. King the other day, just in case you found your penny, if he'd be interested in buying it. He sure would, so give him a call."

My mom gave me a flat gift wrapped in silver paper with a huge red bow. I tore it open while she explained, "I bought this glittery lime-green detective notebook for you two weeks ago. Then, when I saw that you already had the exact same one, I was so disappointed. But the way mysteries seem to find you, I'm sure you'll put it to good use." We hugged and giggled.

Cole said that after he heard Dottie's story about finding the valuable penny, he went home and looked through all the change in his piggy bank.

"It took forever, but I found a 1950-D Jefferson

nickel. On the back, there's a 'D' to the right of Monticello, which was Thomas Jefferson's home. One of the dealers at the coin show gave me ten crisp $1 bills for a 5¢ coin. Can you believe that? "

The welcome bell jingled and a pretty lady in a pink suit walked in.

"I'm sorry," said Wanda, "we're closed for the day."

Donna jumped up from her chair. She was grinning from ear to ear. "Meet my Aunt Lillian, everybody! For her birthday, I made her a coupon for one free car wash. By tonight her car will look like brand new."

"I hear you're a coin collector, too," Dottie said to Aunt Lillian, proud to show off her valuable penny. "Take a look at this 1955..."

"I've been thinking," Nancy said. "I wonder how Dottie's penny got stuck to the tray on the shelf."

"Um, that's a long story I probably should tell you," I began.

"Ah-choo!"

Saved by the sneeze. Choo's paw was on my camera. She was reminding me to take photos for *The Scoop*.

First I took a photo of Otis, his Buried Treasure Cake coin and what was left of the cake.

Then I got everyone to pose together, with Dottie holding up her 1955 double die Lincoln penny.

"OK, on the count of three, everybody smile and say 'Chooooooooo!' Thanks to her sniffer, we've solved another mystery."

Dear Me!
Advice & chitchat

Dear Me,

There's a hubbub* around town and this time it's actually good.

Guess who is going to be the host of The Green Team's new DVD, *The Recycling Starter Kit?*

Yours truly! (I mean "E," of course!)

The opening shot will show the new recycling bins in town. The blue bins are for bottles and cans. The green bins are for newspapers and magazines.

They're already making a big difference (less litter!).

"E" will interview Wanda about how businesses can start recycling.

Wendie will talk about getting recycling going at school.

Then Nancy will be filmed at her house describing a typical day of recycling in the life of a typical American family.

Choo will star in the DVD too, sleeping on her cozy dog bed cushion (the stuffing is now made from recycled plastic bottles).

Signed,
All Smiles ☺

Dear All Smiles,

I have three words for "E": Way to go!

Keep me posted. Good luck!

Glossary

*Many words have more than one meaning. Here are the definitions of words marked with this symbol * (an asterisk) as they are used in sentences.*

backstabber: *a person who talks badly about someone while pretending to be a friend*

beeline: *a fast, straight line from one place to another*

broke: *having very little money*

canine: *dog*

chops: *the area around the mouth*

clanged: *made a loud sound like metal slamming*

concession: *a place where food or items are sold, usually part of an event or larger place*

conclusions, as in "jump to conclusions": *judge without getting the facts first*

contestant: *a person who takes part in a contest*

dachshund: *a dog breed with short legs and a long body*

devouring: *eating hungrily*

disguise: *clothing or costume that makes a person look different than usual*

doubled: *appearing twice*

double die penny: *a penny that clearly shows a double image of all or part of the design*

gadzooks: *a word that shows surprise*

genuine: *real, true*

gourmet: *a person who is a good judge of fine food*

higgledy-piggledy: *jumbled, not in any order*

hightailed: *moved fast*

hip-hop: *a dance performed to a popular style of music that often includes rap*

hodgepodge: *a jumbled mixture of things*

hoo-ha: *a fuss*

hopping, as in "hopping mad": *very angry*

hubbub: *a busy, noisy situation*

hullabaloo: *a noisy fuss*

hunch: *a feeling about something, a guess*

inspired: *caused a creative thought or action*

jitterbug: *a type of fast dance that was popular in the 1940s and performed to swing music*

jostled: *pushed through*

journalists: *people who write or prepare news*

magnifier: *a tool with a lens that makes an object look bigger than it really is and lets tiny details be seen*

mint: *a place where the government makes coins*

motive: *a reason for doing something*

mud, as in "name was mud": *not respected or thought highly of*

muttered: *spoke in a low voice or grumbled*

pickle, as in "in a pickle": *in a difficult and messy situation*

posted, as in "keep me posted": *informed of the latest news*

salsa: *dance performed to a type of Latin-American music*

rocked the boat: *made trouble*

sales pitch: *words said to get someone to buy something*

sidecar: *a small car with wheels that hooks onto a scooter and carries a passenger*

sleuth: *someone who investigates a mystery, a detective*

squirm: *wriggle the body because of a nervous feeling*

suspects: *people who are thought to be guilty*

suspicious: *causing distrust*

undercover: *acting in secret or in a disguise*

unicycle: *a cycle with pedals and a seat, but only one wheel*

vegetarian: *a person who doesn't eat meat, and lives on a diet made up of vegetables, fruits, grains, nuts and sometimes eggs or dairy products*

wingding: *a lively party*

Attention treasure-seekers! Bake a cake with a good-luck coin inside!
Mr. Deebee borrowed this idea from a cake that's been part
of New Year's Day celebrations in Greece and many other cultures
since long ago. Mr. Deebee has a sweet tooth for chocolate,
so this is one of his favorite recipes.

Mr. Deebee's Famous
Buried Treasure Cake

Cake
1 12-ounce can of cola
1 box of chocolate cake mix

Topping
½ cup chocolate chips
½ cup chopped nuts
½ cup coconut

Treasure!
1 quarter wrapped in tinfoil

1. *Ask a treasure-seeker who is an adult to be your assistant baker. Preheat oven to 350°F. Spray a 9" x 13" cake pan with cooking spray.*
2. *In a small bowl, mix chocolate chips, nuts and coconut. Set aside for later.*
3. *In a big bowl, add cola to dry cake mix. (No other ingredients are needed). Mix well.*
4. *Pour mixture into the cake pan. Close your eyes (no peeking!) while your assistant baker pushes the coin into the batter (now its location will be a surprise for you, too).*
5. *Sprinkle chocolate chips, nuts and coconut mixture evenly on top.*
6. *Bake for 35 minutes. Insert a toothpick in the center where there is not a chocolate chip. If there's no batter on it when you pull it out, the cake is done. Let it cool to room temperature. Slice.*
7. ***A super-important reminder: Before serving the cake, make sure your guests know to look for the buried treasure.***
8. *Enjoy—and good luck!*

About the Author

Ever since she can remember, Susan Cappadonia Love has enjoyed reading mysteries. Following their twists and turns makes her stay up far past her bedtime. And trying to figure out whodunit is the icing on the cake. So when she got the chance to write her own mystery, she decided to stir not one, but two cakes into the plot, sweeten it with a dash of girl power and frost it with plenty of friendship.

There's one thing about this mystery that's no mystery at all: the people who had a hand in creating the recipe for Eva's topsy-turvy tale.

For this Susan wishes to thank her husband, Scott, who's chockfull of ideas, her daughter Olivia, who listens to the same chapters over and over and tweaks the wording until it's "just right," and her daughter Sophie, who she can always count on for sound opinions.

Much gratitude also goes to Mylene Vallee at Maison Joseph Battat Ltd. for her creativity and big heart.

Thanks also go to Lano Balulescu, who shared his expertise on the fascinating history of coins as well as coin values in today's market.

Susan Cappadonia Love lives with her family in Milton, Massachusetts. In addition to **The Mystery of the Vanishing Coin**, she has also written two other books in the Our Generation® Series, **Stars in Your Eyes** and **One Smart Cookie**.